FINDING HIM

UNLEASHING HELL BOOK ONE

VIOLA TEMPEST

CONTENTS

Chapter 1   1
Chapter 2   13
Chapter 3   21
Chapter 4   41
Chapter 5   75
Chapter 6   95

UNLEASHING HELL BOOK ONE

FINDING HIM

VIOLA TEMPEST

CHAPTER 1

My name is Bella Nova, and my family and I just moved from Astoria, Oregon to Ojai, California. Why? Because six months ago, I killed someone. Now, before you start judging me, calling me names like a "monster" or a "criminal," know that it wasn't my fault. Turned out, shooting someone in the name of self-defense isn't legal in all counties, and I had to find out the hard way.

But let me take a few steps back. I'm just your normal average seventeen-year-old high school student, nothing more, nothing less. I went to school, got good grades, hung out with my friends, and on weekends, I volunteered at the local animal shelter, where I fed and groomed the animals, preparing them for their new home. All in all, I was the good child, the one who followed all the rules and did as I was told. Unlike my brother, Ace, who ran with all the potheads and stayed out for days at a time.

So, how did I end up in the back of a man's pickup truck? Bound and tied like a chicken ready to be chopped and served? Let's just say, I'm not exactly the smartest grape in the bunch. I excelled when it came to exams and standardized tests, but in the outside world, in reality, my intense lust for any guy who bats his eyes at me, and dreadful fear of ending up alone, usually put me in positions I shouldn't be in.

And Brick Cannon was just too delicious to resist. He came into my high school like a blazing fire, captivating the hearts of everyone he encountered, everyone except for me. And I hated it! I'd watch with envy as he flirted with my best friend,

Chelsea Miller, and it drove me insane whenever he'd just brush right past me to get to her. Like I didn't even exist!

I resented Chelsea for it. Though it wasn't her fault, it also didn't help that she flirted back with him whenever she got the chance, much like all the other girls in my school. He was the most handsome boy I had ever seen in my life, and I'm sure they all thought the same.

But then my luck started to change. Whenever I'd turn around, I'd catch Brick staring at me for a quick second before turning his head away. Was he really looking at me? Or were those eyes just for Chelsea? I second guessed myself for weeks, assuming a boy like him would never be with a girl like me, until he came up to me one day as I was walking home.

"Hey, Bella," he said, flashing me that charming smile, enough to make me swoon. "Whatcha up to?"

I froze. Of course, I did. I'd never spoken to Brick before, always lusting after him from afar, so when he finally came up to me, I didn't know what else to do.

"Hey...," I answered back. "Um, Chelsea isn't here."

He laughed, so heartily that I was sure the entire neighborhood heard.

"Chelsea?" he exclaimed. "Forget about her. It's you I wanna talk to, silly."

My mouth hung open as I pointed to myself. "Me?"

I wasn't sure whether to cheer or faint. After all this time, Brick Cannon, *the* Brick Cannon, actually wanted to talk to me!

"Of course! Why'd you think I hung around Chelsea so much? Because I was too scared to talk to you."

My eyes lit up. I couldn't believe what I was hearing. It was everything I'd always wanted, and I wanted, right then and there, to leap up and throw my arms around his neck.

Brick Cannon. He was interested in me. And I couldn't ask for more.

But although Brick was the greatest, he was definitely not my first... crush, that is. Before my parents met, my mother used to be a bit of a... promiscuous damsel, hitting up clubs every night and bringing home a different boy. I've heard all the stories of her wild teenage years. So have the rest of my family, each one less enthusiastic about my mother's sexuality than I was.

Growing up, I told myself that I would never end up like her, that I would meet the one man of my dreams, get married, and that was it. And I held myself to that promise, until I entered middle school. And everything changed. I had hit puberty and became a woman, and I instantly became hooked on every troublemaker who crossed my path.

At first, it was Billy Styles, my sixth-grade crush whom everyone wanted, and he knew it. It amazed me how much of an ego was able to fit inside such a small package. The girls in my class were just getting over their "cooties" stage, and they all threw themselves at the new "bad boy" who had recently enrolled in our school. And I was no different.

Of course, like all the boys during that time, Billy wanted nothing to do with any of us. Video games and soccer were his calling, not dating, and that only made us all want him that much more.

But that obsession quickly faded when Alex Shaw came into my life two years later. His blonde hair and beautiful blue eyes were enough to make me shiver in all the right places. I wanted nothing more than to be his girlfriend, to lock my arm around his as we stroll to class together.

Unfortunately, his eyes were on Becky Miller, the most popular girl in class, and the one all the boys wanted to date. I didn't stand a chance. I watched in the shadows as Alex and Becky locked their arms together and walked by me every day down the hall. And whenever they kissed, their lips locking and tongues intertwining, I wanted to puke.

I wasn't ugly, per se. I just didn't have *the* look that boys seemed to want. I was just your average girl next door with high standards. I had plenty of suitors knocking on my door, but I wanted the best of the best, the cream of the crop, and I wasn't about to settle for anything less. I'd rather be alone than stoop myself to such level.

Lucky enough for me, Becky Miller's father eventually received an offer he couldn't refuse, and moved his entire family to Chicago, Illinois, forcing Alex and Becky to break up. I smirked as I watched them break it off, making promises to continue their relationship long distant even though everyone knew it wouldn't last, and Alex was in tears as he watched Becky hop in her dad's car and drive away.

And I was right. Less than a week later, Alex turned into a wreck when he saw a picture of his girlfriend on social media with another guy, smiling and laughing as if Alex didn't exist. And guess who was right there to comfort him? Me. No one ever told me that the best time to snag a man is during his lowest point, but that's exactly how I became Alex Shaw's new girlfriend just days later.

We did everything that he and Becky used to do, locking arms as we walked to class, and locking lips while our tongues entangled in a dance. After two months of dating, we even made love for the first time. I'd felt nervous at first, reserved and shy, but he managed to convince me that, if I really loved him, I had to do it for him.

And so, I did, letting my sexual fantasies run wild as he claimed my virginity for himself. I finally had everything I'd ever wanted, and it felt magical.

But maybe all that lust and desire clouded my judgment, because soon, I began to realize that Alex Shaw wasn't who I thought he was. Not at all.

It was our Sophomore year in high school when I finally discovered that my boyfriend had been cheating on me the entire time of our relationship. He had started dating Virginia Wilde soon after Becky left, and was only with me because Virginia refused to put out. "The Middle School Slut," I was known as, and I wanted to die when I found out, overhearing a conversation that Alex was having with his group of friends, bragging about how he'd had sex over thirty-six times.

And I couldn't take it anymore. It was too much. Everywhere I went, guys came up to me, asking me to fuck them, and girls all avoided me, thinking that I'd somehow spread whatever disease I had to them. I felt so alone, so suicidal, that I convinced my parents to transfer me to a new school, in a different county, where no one knew who I was or my past. And that's where I met Brick.

"You like me?" I asked before realizing how awkward and stupid I probably sounded.

All he said was that he wanted to talk to me, and here I was throwing myself at him and expecting something much more.

But he didn't laugh. He didn't point his finger at me and call me an "idiot" like I had expected.

Instead, he rubbed the back of his neck and nodded. "Yeah, I kinda do. Do you maybe wanna grab a soda with me? And it can just be as friends! I don't want to pressure you into anything you're uncomfortable with."

I quickly nodded. "As friends," I said.

I couldn't have him knowing that those few words had already made my panties wet, and I wanted to just tear his clothes off and lick those abs that I imagined he had.

I barely got to know Brick during our date. I was too busy staring into his beautiful eyes, and he was too busy running his fingers up and down my inner thigh. We both wanted each other. Not just as boyfriend and girlfriend, but we both wanted to grab each other by the shirt and make out right then and there in the booth of the diner. And it became much more obvious when he leaned in and kissed me, running his hand up the skirt of my dress and pulling down my cheeky.

"Wait! Not here," I hissed. "There are people here."

Brick looked around and saw three elders slurping on their bowl of soup. Probably all here for the early bird special. His face fell when he tried to persuade me again but was stopped instead.

"I know somewhere we can go. It's old, abandoned, and no one will be there to bother us," he whispered into my ear while nibbling on it.

I eagerly agreed, and he took my hand and led me into his pickup truck. I hesitated and winced when his hand made its way down my underwear, but I really wanted him to like me, so I didn't stop his fingers from exploring. I could feel my body falling for his touch, his sensual touch that made me the wettest I'd ever been. He eventually stopped in front of an old barn that looked like it hadn't been touched in nearly a century and asked me if the place was fine.

But my body had already caved in, and I couldn't even make it out the door of the car before climbing on top of him and unzipping his pants, feeling the girth of him inside of me while I smashed my face against his.

OUR WILD SEXUAL adventure continued for months, fucking everywhere we could, whenever we could, and I had become so head over heels in love with him that I threw all my reserves and common sense right out the window.

Chelsea tried to warn me about Brick, but I refused to listen.

"He's not a good person," she said. "Why do you think I stopped talking to him? All he wants is sex, controlling and manipulating women into giving him what he wants. Don't you see it? Doesn't it seem odd to you that he only ever wants to be around you if you put out?"

But I just rolled my eyes at her. Chelsea had been my best friend ever since I transfer to Astoria High, but there was no chance in Hell that I was going to let her come between me and the boy of my dreams.

"You're just jealous that he wants me and not you. Brick loves me," I said back to her. "I love him, and we're going to be together forever."

I should've listened to Chelsea when I had the chance. Even my mother, the Queen of Lust, tried to warn me about Brick Cannon. There was a certain sense of evil in his eyes that I'd failed to notice until it was too late.

He had killed before, he told me when I ultimately found myself being held captive in that abandoned barn. And I wouldn't be his last, just another pawn to satisfy his craving as he made his way across the country. And here I was thinking Alex Shaw was bad. Never did I imagine being manipulated and kidnapped by a fucking serial killer.

And that's how I ended up in California. On the run for shooting a man before he had a chance to shoot me first. They may come after me. After all, I *had* committed a crime. But they might not. I had played the role of a vigilante, and shooting Brick Cannon only meant sparing the lives of many other women he had planned on conquering.

I could sit here and think about all the possibilities of my fate, but I'd much rather tune them all out and forget about my past. I have a new life now in Ojai, and though it seems like I'm always running from one problem to another, these were all life-or-death situations. I had no other choice.

CHAPTER 2

O jai, California is a small valley just north of Los Angeles, where people are both friendly and superstitious. Although they'd do anything, even things out of their way, to help a newcomer settle in and make this town their home, they'd never refrain from telling their own tales of how Ojai is haunted. No one knows why or what it's haunted by; they just know that once every thousand years, something strange happens to the town of Ojai, a sort of vibration, followed by an aura that many of the elders deem as "evil."

Some of the more superstitious folks think it's a sign from God, his way of warning the residents that the end is near and to get their shit together before the whole world collapses. Others just brush it off as another earthquake, something that's common to residents of California, given how it resides on the San Andreas Fault.

But whatever it is, no one has ever lived long enough after the incident to carry on the message. Maybe the world really does end once every thousand years. Maybe God does open the Gate of Heaven and sends the good ones up. Or maybe, everyone in this town is full of nonsense and bullshit.

"You folks better be careful," one of our neighbors warns us as my father pulls into the driveway of our new home. "It's another thousand years again. Who knows what, or who, will come upon us this year? My husband, Charlie, and I have been preparing for over a year now."

"Preparing?" my mother asks, pulling a suitcase from the trunk.

"For the apocalypse!"

That's when the husband walks out. "Oh, don't listen to Betsy. It's all just nonsense. There's no apocalypse. It's just a little vibration, nothing to be too concerned about."

"But we do have that bomb shelter, you know, just in case." Betsy points out to Charlie.

"That's true, we do. I doubt we'll need it, but it never hurts to have a backup."

"Thanks for the heads up," my father says as he walks into the home.

"Anytime, neighbors!" Betsy calls out after him. "And if you folks need a place to stay during the apocalypse, our shelter has plenty of room!"

"It's not an apocalypse, Betsy!" Charlie angrily storms inside and slams the door behind him.

Betsy turns to the rest of us and apologizes. "Oh, don't mind him. Charlie's always cranky in the morning, but you'll get used to him. Anyway, welcome to Ojai, and be safe out there. If the apocalypse doesn't kill us, some of the weirdos who cross through here from LA most likely will. It's a dangerous, dangerous world." She finishes and proceeds to walk back into her home.

"Is there really an apocalypse coming?" Ace asks

our parents, plopping his ass down on the couch, still wrapped and sealed.

"Nah," my father says. "Don't mind them. They're old. They don't know what they're talking about. An apocalypse every thousand years? A sign from God? Come on, it's all a bunch of rumors. Probably to scare away newcomers." He sits down beside Ace. "Ojai's a great town. I've heard nothing but good things about this place. Don't let our crazy neighbors get to you."

"Your father's right, kids. Nothing's going to happen. The apocalypse is nothing but a rumor. Now, go set up your rooms. You both start school tomorrow," Mom chimes in.

I pick up my bags and head up to my room. The stairs creak as I walk, and the flimsy railing makes me wonder whether I'm safer skipping it altogether. The house is old, a Victorian-style home, probably from the early 1800s. It smells of dust and old people, and I wouldn't be surprised if I find several rats living up in the attic.

Ace had already claimed his room by the time I make my way upstairs, belly flopped on his floor mattress while playing on his phone. I have no choice but to choose the other one, the smaller, much smaller, bedroom. It's always the same wherever we go. Ace would get the better option. Perks of being the older one, I guess.

I never liked change, but this is one I desperately needed. I can't go back to Astoria. Too much history back there that I'd rather forget. And Chelsea, I never got the chance to tell her that I was moving. But it wasn't like we'd really spoken since I ignored her for Brick. I sigh. That's my life, always making bad choices and screwing everything up.

After throwing my suitcase onto the carpeted floor, I walk over to the windowsill, twisting the pentagram ring on my right ring finger. Brick had given it to me on our third date, said it suited my style, and for me to cherish it forever. Now, I keep thinking whether he just swiped it off a dead girl. But still, it holds sentimental value. I think I'll keep it for now.

The wind is blowing heavily outside, splatters of rain whacking hard against the pane. I look outside, and even amid the gloomy and depressing weather, the townspeople don't seem to mind. Yellow coats and purple umbrellas line the streets, and cars slowly glide along the roads as if no one is ever in a rush.

"Bella! Ace!" I hear my mother cry out. "Time for lunch!"

I spin around to head back downstairs. I can

always unpack later. The day is long, and the night is longer. There's really no point in rushing. Besides, I could hear my stomach growl the entire ride down. I need to eat something before I pass out.

When I walked into the kitchen, Mom's already setting the table with plates of turkey and brie sandwiches for everyone, with a large bowl of tomato soup sitting in the center.

"Juice?" she asks me as I sit down.

"No, thanks. I'll just have some water." I reach over in front of me and pour myself a glass.

"Pour me some of that, will ya?"

I look up, and Ace walks in, sitting himself down also, phone still in hand. I roll my eyes at him, but he doesn't seem to notice. Hell, he never seems to notice.

"Take mine," I respond, handing the glass over to him before returning to pour myself another. "Where's Dad?" I ask Mom.

"Unloading the rest of the trunk. He'll be in soon."

I watch as Mom finishes wiping her hands on a towel and grabs a few utensils from the drawer.

Such a motherly figure. It's hard to believe that she once worked in a strip club.

"So," Mom asks after taking a few bites of her

sandwich. "You two ready for your first day of school?"

"Why do I have to go to the same school as Bella here, anyway?" Ace whines. "She'll just embarrass me. No one wants to be seen with their kid sister."

"Hey! You're no prize, either!" I retort.

"Stop it!" Dad throws his sandwich on his plate and interjects. "We've talked about this. Villanova Prep is the best school in the area. And your mother and I want you both to have the best education we can afford. So, unless you want to end up on the streets of LA with all the addicts on Skid Row, I suggest you keep your mouth shut and enjoy what you're given."

"What's wrong, Bella?" Mom asks when she notices me picking at my sandwich instead of eating it.

I shrug, and even though I'm trying to focus on Mom, I can still hear my father and Ace bickering beside me.

"What if nothing changes? It's a new school, a new town, but what if my past comes back to haunt me? What if I fall for another guy who ruins me?"

Mom places her sandwich back on her plate and comes over to sit beside me. She wraps her arms around mine and pulls me in for a hug.

"Remember what we talked about, honey. Whatever happened in the past, stays in the past. Learn from it. Grow from it. I trust that things will be different for you this time. We left Astoria for a reason, so you can start over. Don't let it all be for nothing."

"Yeah," Ace yells over. "Don't kill anyone this time."

My face immediately turns red, and all the pain I had tried so hard to suppress comes rushing back. I push my chair back and throw the rest of my sandwich at him. "You jerk!"

Tears continue to pour from my eyes as I run upstairs into my room and slam the door. I can hear my mom scolding him for what he had said, but the tears won't stop flowing.

I'm a monster. A murderer. A slut. All that and more that I will never be able to truly escape from.

CHAPTER 3

The next morning, my alarm blares before the sun's even out. I wake up with tired eyes and a pounding headache. I had tossed and turned all night, the flashbacks of my past creeping into my nightmare. Sometimes when I sleep, I can still see the stains of Brick's blood on my hands, the life of another person gone because of me.

It's a blemish that will forever be part of my record, a brand that I can never run from no matter what I end up accomplishing.

How could someone so handsome, so charming, so sexy, turn out to be such a monster? I'll also always wonder how our relationship would've turned out if he didn't turn out to be a serial killer. Three kids, twin girls and one boy, a small cottage in the woods with a small pond behind it. That's how I would've liked that relationship to have turned out.

Brick Cannon was my greatest love, a wild adventure I'll never forget, and even though he ultimately died by my own hands, he'll always have a special place in my heart, the gold standard for every boy who comes after him.

I glance over at the uniform laying on my bed, a white button-down blouse, a blue plaid mini skirt, and blue and white saddle shoes, topped with matching knee-length socks. I sigh again. I never had to wear a uniform before, but maybe this is better. Maybe forcing everyone to dress the same will prevent some girls from getting all the hot guys. I quickly shake my head at that thought. No, that can't be my focus. Not anymore. It's done nothing but get me into trouble.

As I strip off my pajamas, letting it all fall to the

floor, I can't help but stare at the scar on my left arm, my mind flashing back again. Brick had left it when his nails clawed into me while I tried to escape, ripping into my flesh and pulling me back. The excruciating pain was too much to bear, but I knew I had to keep pulling away if I wanted even a slim chance of getting away. It hadn't quite healed properly, a constant reminder of my dangerous rendezvous with love, but somehow, I preferred it this way.

The blue plaid skirt didn't quite reach the length I had wanted it to when I pulled it on. I can still see the bite marks left on my inner thigh from when Brick nibbled on them after going down on me during one of our passionate affairs. They were innocent at first. "Love bites" as I call them. But then he got rough, aggressive, and now, I have three sets of teeth marks imprinted onto my skin.

After pulling on my socks, I walk over to my vanity and grab my concealer. It's the best thing I can think of with such last-minute notice. But still, despite how much of the cream I plaster on, I can still see the faint marks sitting there, mocking me.

"Bella! You ready up there? We're gonna miss the bus!" Ace calls up from the living room.

Fuck. I get up and quickly grab my backpack

from my closet. It's filled with nothing but a couple pencils and a small notebook, but what else am I supposed to bring with me on my first day of school? I then quickly climb into my shoes, grab my phone, and hurry down the stairs, where I find Ace standing there with his arms crossed over his chest.

"About time," he huffs.

I mumble "sorry" and follow him out the door to the bus stop, which is only a few feet from our house.

"You better stay away from me at school," Ace mutters in my direction. "There, we're complete strangers. Got it? There, you're not my kid sister."

"Stop calling me a kid! And fine, I don't want to be associated with an asshole, anyway."

The both of us remain silent during the rest of the wait. So quiet that I can hear him typing away at his phone while I look around at all the yellow coats and purple umbrellas walking from left to right, and vice versa. It sure gets rainy in this town, and it still surprises me how the folks around here can remain so optimistic even as they're being drenched.

Minutes later, the yellow bus pulls up. Ace gets on first, finding a seat in the back, while I drag behind and scoot into a seat near the front, alone. The rest of the kids on the bus look like us, white button-down shirts with blue plaid skirts for the girls, and khaki pants for the boys.

The ride down the road is bumpy, hitting a pothole every time we pass a light or a stop sign. I can hear Ace in the back chatting it up with another boy, laughing and joking around, while I remain silent with my earbuds in, trying to ease the anxiety creeping up on me.

The town of Ojai just seems so strange the more I look at it. More and more yellow coats with purple umbrellas grace the streets, with people still unfazed by the harsh weather that's pouring down on them. And why are they all dressed the same? It's like I'd left a town of normalcy and moved into some sort of cult.

When the driver stops, a bunch more students hop on. One of them is a boy about my age with dark brown hair and emerald green eyes. I can feel my body tingling when he decides to sit next to me.

"Hey, I'm Daven. Daven Porter," he says to me, extending a hand out.

I pull my own hand out from the pocket of my blazer and shake it. "Bella Nova."

"Bella, I like that name. It's very sweet." He points to my right hand. "Cool ring, by the way."

He flashes a smile at me, one that makes me want

to just collapse in his arms. But no, I can't. Not again. Before moving to Ojai, I made a promise to myself and my mother that I would try and restrain myself more when it comes to boys. I can't let myself fall for the first one who says I have a sweet name.

"Thanks," I reply, quickly pulling my hand away.

"So, Bella, are you new? I haven't seen you around town before, and I know everyone. My father's the town mayor, so it's my duty to know all the residents here."

I nod. The mayor's son? Even hotter. "My family just moved here from Oregon yesterday."

"Oregon, interesting. Portland? My parents like to take my sister and I to Mount Hood every winter to ski. We always have so much fun there."

I shake my head. Even though I'd lived in Oregon my entire life, I never really left Astoria. There was just never any reason to.

"Astoria."

"Never heard of it."

"It's a little coastal town in northern Oregon, near the border of Washington. Many people don't know about it."

"Why the move here?"

I'm starting to realize that this isn't just another

two-second conversation, that Daven is going to keep talking to me even though I have earbuds in. Slowly, I pull them from my ears, grip them into a ball, and tuck them into the side pocket of my backpack.

"It's a long story," I manage to get out without choking up. "We just wanted a change, that's all."

I'm trying to escape my past, not relive it. No way in Hell am I going to disclose the story of my entire tragic past to some cute boy I just met.

"Let me guess, a memory you'd rather just forget?" He turns and smiles at me, his eyes showing a complete understanding to my situation.

"Something like that." I smile back.

When the bus finally pulls up to the front of the school, Daven escorts me off the bus.

"How would you like a personal tour guide on your first day? I know how daunting it can be arriving on a campus you're not familiar with. Also, it doesn't help that this campus has eight buildings." He chuckles and pulls out his phone to check the time.

"I'd love that."

I turn around and see Ace still chatting it up with the boy from the bus. I'm not sure what he's up to, but I bet it's nothing good.

"Come on!" Daven gestures to me as the bell rings, and I follow him into the main building.

Despite being over a thousand miles away, Villanova Prep looks just like Astoria High, the school separated into their own cliques, from the popular cheerleaders to the burly jocks to the stoners sheltered in the janitor's closet and getting high during study period. Ace and the boy from the bus walk straight into that one.

Immediately, I know there's a slim chance that I'll fit in with any of these crowds. I'll probably just resort to eating lunch alone in a bathroom stall, much like Cady Heron in Mean Girls, when no one at her new school wanted her.

"Hey, Daven!"

"Looking sharp, Daven. Looks like you worked out this summer."

"Sexy as ever, Daven. I'll see you around."

When we walk in, all the girls in the hallway start flirting with him, like he's a piece of meat thrown into a pit full of lions. It's clear that Daven Porter is the Brick Cannon of this school, the Alex Shaw, the Billy Styles. It's no wonder why I found myself instantly attracted to him.

"Now, now, ladies, settle down. There's only so

much of me. I can't give my attention to all of you," he says to them.

"Aw, then at least choose one of us!" A blonde girl starts to whine. "It's Junior year. Don't you think it's about time that you stop being single and choose one of us? Preferably me?"

He chuckles and turns to her. "Stephanie, Stephanie, Stephanie. You know better than anyone that I can't do that. If I date one of you, the rest of you will just get angry. What'll happen to your friendship then?" He reaches out a hand and tucks a strand of hair behind Stephanie's ear, making her blush. "Besides, I'm sort of enjoying all this attention. Makes me feel special."

"You *are* special!" Stephanie agrees, blushing again with the rest of the group giddy behind her.

"Anyway, I should really get going." Then he points to me. "This is Bella. She's new, and I want you all to be nice to her. Got it?"

As they all nod, Daven leads me away. I can hear a sigh of relief coming from him. And I don't blame him. If I had that many people fawning over me, I'd feel stressed out, too. But then again, it's a problem I'll never have to worry about. I'm always the one chasing, never the one being chased.

"Is it true?" I ask as we walk down the hall in the opposite direction.

Daven looks at me and smiles. I'll never grow tired of that charming smile. "Is what true?"

"That the only reason you're single is because you don't want them to kill each other."

"Ha! Of course not. It was the only thing I could think of to let her down easy. They're all obsessed with me, or more so, they're all obsessed with my father's money. The girls in this school are all the same. Instead of trying to succeed and make their own money, they'd rather chase after someone with a rich family. It's a bit sickening, actually. And there's definitely no chance that I'd ever go out with one of them, especially not the cheerleaders. They're all ditzes."

"Wow, I never would've guessed how you truly feel based on that conversation back there. At first, I thought you were just—"

"Shallow?" he finishes for me. "I can see why you might think that. But it's all for show. I have a reputation to uphold, after all. If word gets out that the mayor's son is walking around school being an obnoxious dick, he'd lose all his supporters. Plus, I'm student body president. I need to keep up this façade if I have any chance of winning again next year."

"So... would you ever date? Even if it's not one of them?"

He whips his head over and grins at me. "Why? Are you interested?"

And that's when my face turns red as I quickly force myself to shake my head and look away. "Just curious, that's all."

Out of the corner of my eye, I notice that he quickly turns his head away also, rubbing the back of his neck with his hand and letting out a small chuckle. "Yeah... yeah, same. Just curious." He looks down at his watch, probably for some sort of distraction from this conversation. "We should really get going. I don't want you to be late for your first class. It wouldn't be very student body president of me if I let that happen."

His grabs my hand and picks up his steps, my little feet fiddling behind, but I don't mind.

Am I falling for him already? It's only the first day of school, and I'm already getting myself in trouble?

During lunch, I can hear the whispers and laughter directed at me when I walk into the cafeteria. It's beginning to grow clear to me that these people are not welcoming of newcomers, for fear of them disrupting their little cliques. Some things just never change.

After grabbing my lunch, I walk past the cheer-leaders, with Stephanie Grimes, the obvious Queen Bee, cackling and hissing insults in my direction. At that moment, I want nothing more than to take my tray and dump it over her fresh perm, watching the milk and yogurt drip down her face and ruining her makeup.

But I can't. I have to remain strong and restrain myself to avoid my parents sending me to yet another school. So, instead, I grit my teeth, grinding them hard against each other to prevent myself from saying something I'd regret.

SEVERAL HOURS LATER, I find myself anxiously staring at the clock, waiting for the final bell to ring. My first day at Villanova Prep isn't anything to brag about or take home. It's not like it's anything I haven't experienced before. The same crap as my old schools. Stuck up girls, and brawly, dumb meatheads. And although Daven has been nice to me, I still ate lunch alone. Ace was nowhere to be seen, not even in the cafeteria. I just hope he shows up for the bus.

"Hey, Bella!" I hear someone shout from behind me.

Thinking it's Ace, I plaster on a stern look on my face before turning around, just to see Daven running toward me. I quickly force my stern face into a smile.

"Hey, Daven."

"How was your first day? I'm sorry I wasn't around much. The student council had meetings all day, and between that and classes, I barely had any time for myself."

"It's fine." I shrug.

I can't tell him the truth, that I had to eat alone, that I had to thwart the evil stares of the cheerleaders and the inappropriate advances of the jocks. I can't have him knowing what a shitty first day I had, and how Daven's probably my only friend. I can't have him thinking I'm a loser.

"You're not mad at me, are you? Because I wasn't there?"

I shake my head. "No, of course not. It's been a long day, that's all."

He let out a sigh. "Whew! That's a relief!"

"Does it bother you if people are mad at you?"

"Nope!" He puts his hands on my shoulders. "It bothers me if *you're* mad at me."

As he says that, a wave of awkward tension washes over us, and silence lingers in the air for a few brief moments.

"Bella! Let's go!" The shrieking sound of Ace's voice breaks the strain between us, and I couldn't be happier.

"I have to go," I finally manage to say.

"I'll see you tomorrow?"

As I nod, I can hear Ace shouting my name again, so loud that I'm sure the rest of the school can hear him, too. But Ace has never been one to care whether the world sees him as a lunatic. He's just Ace, a free-spirited, obnoxious loud mouth.

During the ride home, I pop in my earbuds and slowly let my mind wander away. One day down, just a hundred and seventy-nine left to go. It's going to be a rough year for sure. The rain continues to pour down on the roads outside, the yellow coats and purple umbrellas still passing by each other with almost robotic waves of hello. There's definitely something going on with this town. Or maybe, I'm just not used to all the friendliness.

Suddenly, I feel a slight tap on my shoulder. Expecting it to be Ace, I whip my head around, but am greeted by no one. There isn't even anyone sitting directly behind me, and I start to turn red. After the day I had today, I'm just not in the mood for any pranks, especially not from Ace. There's only so much I can deal with in one day.

When the bus arrives at our stop, I grab my bag and walk off, Ace skipping behind toward me.

"Why so fast? Got someone else you gotta murder?"

I stop, my rage growing even more intense. "What the hell's your problem?"

He backs away. "Whoa, chill the fuck out. It's just a joke!"

"Not that! Why'd you tap me on the bus earlier and just disappear? Is that supposed to be funny?"

"What the hell are you talking about? I was nowhere near you."

"Just lay off, Ace. Just lay off!"

I angrily storm away, in the opposite direction of home. I don't care that it's pouring, and I'm getting drenched. I don't care that Mom will throw a fit because I'm late. I don't care that I'm wandering around a town I barely know all alone. I hate it here!

I can hear my phone ring in my pocket, but I just ignore it. It's probably Ace, calling to make sure I'm not dead so Dad won't kill him for showing up to the house without his sister. Whatever. He deserves whatever he has coming his way.

There's a canal near our home that I hadn't noticed when we first moved here. I was too busy having nightmares about my past in the car to focus on my surroundings. But it's beautiful, even in the midst of a rainstorm. The green lily pads floating on the naturally blue water, such a beautiful and calming sight to see. I can just sit here for hours staring out into its beauty, if the pouring rain wouldn't get me sick.

But still, it doesn't hurt to live out that dream a little. Dropping my bag down on the wet asphalt, I draw my blazer over my head and plop myself onto the concrete. The puddle of water soak through my skirt, but I don't care. With all the craziness in my life, I just need a moment of peace to forget about it all.

What am I doing with my life, anyway? I can't keep forcing my family to move every time I fuck up. I should be in prison right now, not a prep school. My parents had been understanding enough to take me away, but that also makes them accomplices, and I can't have them keep covering up for my falls.

I lean back on my hands, my fingers brushing against gravel and rocks. Gosh, I can't even remember the last time I've felt so connected with nature. Fishing for a fairly large rock, I pick it up and chuck it into the canal, the sound of the quiet plop like music to my ears.

Brick and I went by the bay once, his favorite spot near Youngs Bay that he said he'd like to go to every now and then to relax and clear his mind. It's a large empty field of absolute nothingness, a quiet and isolated part of town that barely gets any traffic. I remember the day he suggested a picnic during a sunny afternoon, beer in hand with a basket full of sandwiches and fruit. Though, it wasn't like we really did any eating. One beer in, and Brick was already all over me, climbing on top of me and tearing my clothes off. Looking back now, I wonder if that was actually a spot he took all his victims. Even the thought of it sends chills up my body.

Then I hear another plop, the sound of another rock splashing into the canal. Is someone else here? I turn my head to look around, curious to see who else is crazy enough to stand here, throwing rocks in the dead of a thunderstorm.

But I can't see anyone. Maybe it's because of the haze from the storm, or they're hiding in the shadows somewhere that I'm not aware of, but to me, I'm all alone. Strange. It better not be Ace. But then again,

Ace would never be out here. He spends all his time indoors, either playing video games or getting high. Nature sickens him, his own words.

The rain continues to pour down even harder; time for me to go if I don't want to get sick. I press my hands against the concrete to hoist myself up, grab my backpack, and start heading home.

When I get back, I'm lucky enough to find that Mom and Dad are still at work. Ace is home, his door shut with his usual "Bella not allowed" sign stuck on his bedroom door. I roll my eyes. Whatever. I don't need him.

So, I walk into my own room, closing the door behind me before changing into some dry clothes. Sweatpants and an oversized sweater are usually my go-to. Why sacrifice comfort to look pretty for no one? I then throw myself onto my bed and pull out my phone. A missed call from Daven. So, it was him who called earlier, not Ace. How'd he even get my number?

Nonetheless, I decide to call him back. There's never any harm in seeing what a cute boy wants. For now, anyway.

"Hello?" A deep voice picks up on the other line.

"Hey, Daven. It's me, Bella."

There's a pause on the other end.

"Bella! I'm so glad you called back! I was beginning to get a little worried."

Worried? Was he worried about me? Does he care about me?

"Sorry, I was busy earlier. I must've missed it. How'd you get my number, anyway?"

He chuckles, and I can tell that he's smiling on the other line. "I guess that's a little creepy, isn't it? I forgot to mention. I also work in the school office. I pretty much have access to everyone's records."

"You're not going to come over here and murder me, are you?" I joke.

"Nah, no way! You're too pretty to die. I just feel really bad about not being there for you on your first day, and it felt like our conversation earlier ended on a sour note. I don't want you to hate me, Bella."

"Why do you care so much about what I think of you?"

I can tell where this conversation is heading, and even though I knew I shouldn't, I can't stop myself. Daven is just too charming.

"Because... because I like you, Bella. You're different from all the other girls, especially those ditzy cheerleaders. You're real, and super, super pretty."

I put down my phone and smile, hands over my

mouth to prevent a squeal of excitement from coming out.

"Would you like to go out with me, Bella? Just one date? And if you hate it, I promise to never bother you again."

I nod, but then quickly realize that he can't see it. Clearing my throat to avoid sounding too enthusiastic, I whisper, "Yes, I'd love to go out with you."

"Oh, wow, I'm so excited that you said yes! Honestly, I'd never asked anyone out before. I never found someone who seemed like a right fit until I met you. I was so nervous that you'd say no. How about tomorrow after school? Meet up after our last class for burgers and milkshakes?"

"Sounds like a plan," I whisper again before hanging up.

I can't keep myself from smiling from ear to ear. I have a date with Daven Porter, the cutest guy in school *and* the son of the mayor. It's risky. Daven seems nice enough on the outside, someone reputable enough to not put me in a position where I have to move again. But then again, that's what I thought when I dated all the others.

Just one date. One date can't hurt, and if I start to see any sign of evil, then I'll immediately cut it off. It's a plan I'm sure I can commit to.

CHAPTER 4

"Brick, what is all this? Who are all these women?" I turned around to face him, holding a stack of photos of different women, all either partially undressed or completely naked.

He winked at me. "Nice collection, isn't it? You'll be part of it very soon. Isn't that exciting?"

"What are you talking about? Part of what?"

Suddenly, he pulled a knife out from behind his back, the blade shiny and the tip sharp. He had an evil look on his face, so evil that I couldn't look away but also couldn't look directly at. And before I knew it, he lunged at me, piercing my wrists with his hands while holding the blade in his mouth.

"What are you doing? Get off! Get the fuck off me!" I screamed and tried to pry myself away from his grip, but he was twice the size of me. It'd be a miracle for me to escape.

"It's what you wanted, right?" he asked, his voice menacing and mocking. "To be with me forever? Well, this is your chance!"

I continued to kick and squirm, whatever I could to escape from his grasp. I could smell the disgusting stench of coffee and cigarette on his breath, and it made me want to vomit.

"No! Stop it, Brick! Let me go!"

My foot eventually found its way to the lower half of his body, and with one swift kick, he came tumbling down, his hands grasped around his balls. I quickly pulled myself up and started running, tripping over myself from the distress and distraught. But I could still hear him coming after me from behind, coming in fast, and I knew I had to bolt.

Another trip later, I found a gun, a small pistol below my feet, and I knew it was my saving grace. I turned around and pointed it at him.

"Stop, Brick! Come any closer, and I'll shoot." My voice was shaking, my confidence hesitant, and he could sense it.

It didn't faze him one bit, and he grunted and charged closer to me. I closed my eyes, afraid for my life, and pulled the trigger. A loud thump was soon heard against the ground, and when I opened my eyes again, there he was, lying face down, blood pouring from his body.

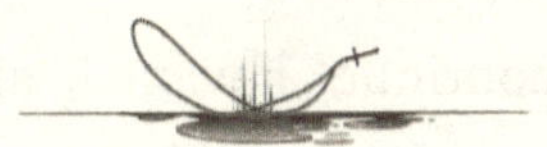

My ALARM RINGS, and I spring out of bed, gasping for air. It's all just a dream, a horrible, horrible dream. I don't expect these memories to stop appearing any time soon, but just for a night or two, I'd like a break so I can at least get some sleep.

I can see Daven standing in the front yard of the main building when I got off the bus. He walks over to me, greets me with a hug, and pulls a yellow daisy from behind his back.

"For you." He smiles.

"What's this for?"

"Our date later, silly! You didn't expect me to show up empty-handed, did you? I wouldn't be a gentleman if I did."

I smile, my heart beating even faster when he grabs onto my hand and squeezes it tight. "You're a gentleman?"

"Father taught me well. I'm as gentle as any man can be!"

He starts to laugh, and I join in alongside him.

That's when he briefly stops and looks over at me. "You're so cute when you laugh," and leans over to kiss me on the cheek.

I let him continue. I want it all, his touch, his affection, his everything, and he knows it.

When we both enter through the front doors and into the hallway, I can feel all eyes on us, especially the death glares of the girls. Rather than their usual flirtatious greetings to Daven, it's obvious that they want to cut in between us and tear us apart. And no one wants to do that more than Stephanie.

"What in the actual fuck, Daven?" she asks. "I thought you said you're not dating anyone!"

"I'm not," Daven answers her, gripping my hand tighter.

"Oh, really, then what the hell is this?!" Her gaze starts to travel down, stopping at where our hands joined.

"Oh, this? Bella and I aren't dating. Not yet, anyway. Our first one's later this afternoon."

I'm actually surprised by how nonchalantly he said that, like he doesn't care whether he offends anyone. That only turns me on even more.

But I can't say the same for Stephanie.

"Dating?! Her?! Why? She's... she's so... plain," she finally finishes, wrinkles forming on her forehead from the look of disgust that she throws over at me. "Wouldn't you rather go out with someone pretty and popular, like me?" She spins around, her cheer-leader outfit flying out and exposing the underwear she's wearing beneath it. All the boys around her can't stop staring, but Daven doesn't seem to pay any attention.

"I'll stick with Bella," he calmly says and looks over at me.

He then leans down and kisses my cheek again, my face turning red.

It made all the other girls fume. I can almost see the smoke coming out from their ears, and for once, I feel less alone. I have Daven. If no one else, the one person who actually matters is here for me.

AFTER SCHOOL, Daven and I met up by the flag pole for our date. He gave me another hug, longer this time, and we both walked to the diner that's close to campus. He told me to choose a booth while he went up to order our food: the greasiest cheeseburger for each of us and chocolate shakes.

"I'm so glad you're not vegan," he says with a mouthful of burger. "You have no idea how obsessed everyone in that school is about eating strictly vegan, gluten-free, non-GMO, sugar-free, keto-based foods."

"They eat air?" I ask lightheartedly.

That made him laugh. "Pretty much!"

"Can I ask? What is it about me that made you want to go out with me? I'm not pretty like Stephanie and all the other cheerleaders. They had a point. I'm really just sort of plain."

"I don't think that at all." He scoots out from his side of the booth and joins me, pressing his body next to me and wrapping his arm around my shoulders. "I think you're way prettier and way better than them. You're humble, real, like I can be myself around you without worrying that you're only in it for the money."

"I don't care about money."

"Exactly! And I sensed that when I first met you. You're just so unique and special, Bella."

I turn my head slightly and can see him staring at me, as if he's peering through my eyes and into my soul. "Why are you staring at me like that?"

"Sorry." He blushes. "But I'm just wondering what it would feel like to kiss you right now."

"You can if you want," I reply shyly.

And just like that, he wraps his other arm around me and pulls me in, staring into my eyes a bit more before leaning in with his face. His lips taste sweet, and although he said he'd never dated before, his lips say otherwise as they caress against mine. I find myself melting like butter into his arms, my body falling prey to the power he seems to have over me.

"Wow," he whispers when he pulls away slightly.

And before I have a chance to say anything, he pulls back in and begins caressing my lips again. I've had many kisses in my past, some great, others pretty terrible. But this? This is definitely my best to date.

After we finished the rest of our food, Daven insists that he walks me to the bus stop before parting ways. "I want to make sure you're safe. I want to protect you."

He kisses me softly on the lips again and grabs my hand to leave. The storm is still pouring when we walk out, and I continue to watch the yellow coats and purple umbrellas cross our path. That's when Daven pulls out his own purple umbrella.

"What's with the purple umbrella?" I ask. "Why does everyone around here dress the same when it rains?"

"You know, I've actually never noticed that. My guess is that yellow coats and purple umbrellas are all we sell around here. People will have to drive all the way to LA if they want a different color, and it's definitely not worth all the trouble."

"That explains a lot. I was starting to think I'm going crazy."

"You're definitely not going crazy."

He pops open his umbrella and pulls me in under it, shielding me from the wet droplets falling from the sky. I feel safe in his arms, like he can never do anything wrong and will never hurt me. When we finally get to the bus stop, he turns to me and asks.

"Bella, I really enjoyed our date. Like, really. And I know it's only our first, and we still have a lot to learn about each other, but would you like to be my girlfriend?"

Boy, he moves fast! And here I am thinking I'm the only one. I made a promise to myself that I wouldn't date at all for the remainder of high school, but Daven is someone that even my strict father would approve of. It's just too hard to turn down.

"I'd love to."

He kisses me again, his arms wrapping around my waist and holding me close until we both hear the bus pull up.

"Call me when you get home?" he whispers.

I nod again and climb onto the bus, waving goodbye to my new boyfriend as the bus drives away.

During dinner later that night, my mother notices the change in my attitude.

"Looks like someone had a good day today. Bella, honey, why are you smiling so much?"

I can't tell her about Daven, not yet, anyway. It'll bring up too many questions, and it'll only make my father throw a fit about having to move again.

"I bet it's a boy," Ace chimes in. "Bella's only ever happy when she has a new boy toy."

I grab a bread roll and throw it at him.

"Ace! Be nice! And Bella, stop throwing your

dinner." My father looks up from his plate long enough to lecture us before returning to his steak.

"It's nothing, Mom. I just had a good day at school."

Ace is onto me, and I can't have him exposing me to our parents before I'm ready.

"Well, I'm glad, sweetie. It's good to see that things are turning around for you."

"I still bet it's a boy," Ace mumbles under his breath.

"Ace!" Mom hisses at him, shutting him up during the rest of dinner.

I can hardly fall asleep later that night. I can't stop thinking about my new school life now that I'm Daven Porter's girlfriend. I'll definitely be treated differently, by the cheerleaders especially. But for once, I'll be part of the popular crowd, part of the table at lunch that everyone wants to sit at. For once, I'll actually be someone.

I decide to send one final text to Daven, telling him that I can't wait to see him tomorrow, before climbing into bed and pulling the sheets over my head. Maybe with this new change in mood, I'll finally stop having nightmares about my past.

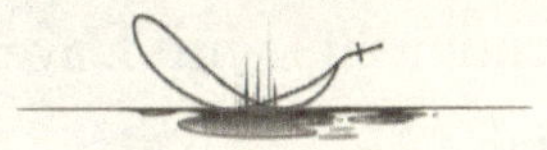

"Bella, Bella Nova," a mysterious and deep voice calls out to me.

"What? Who is it? Who's here?"

I wake up, and while I'm still wearing my pajamas, I'm no longer in my bed. Instead, I find myself lying in some sort of cave, like a hole that has been dug underground and is beginning to heat up like a sauna.

"Hello?" I call out again.

I place a hand on the ground. "Ouch!" The black asphalt feels nothing like the ground by the canal. This feels almost... squishy? Warm and squishy, like there's a pool of lava sitting beneath it.

As I look around, I see a dark and shadowy figure fly by my vision. I can't quite make out what it is, but whatever it is, its skin is dark as night, and I'm pretty sure I saw horns. Maybe a ram? Or a different type of animal?

I've enjoyed a hike or two in my lifetime. Growing up in Oregon, I sort of had to if I wanted to spend time outdoors. But never have I, or will I, ever dreamt of spending the night in a cave with a wild animal. I still have so much to live for, so much to see. And my relationship with Daven, I can't die just when it's starting!

I quietly stand up, brushing the dirt off my sweatpants and straightening out my sweater. What is that? Dare I follow it? Or will it jump out and eat me alive? My mind tells me to stay put until someone comes to save me, but my body is curious to see what the dark figure around the corner is. Without being aware of it, my legs start moving, moving and moving toward the large rock in the corner where the figure seemed to have bolted off to.

But then I hear another whisper, a female voice this time. "Bella, Bella, wake up."

"Mom?"

"Bella, Bella, it's time to wake up," the voice says again, followed by the blaring sound of my alarm.

"I'm up! I'm up!" I spring up on my bed and shout.

Mom looks at me, startled by my sudden reaction. "Bad dream, honey?"

I look around, finding myself back in my own bedroom. It was all just a dream, a strangely realistic dream. "Yeah, something like that."

When I finished getting ready and came down-stairs, Ace is already gone. He had taken the bus alone this morning since Daven called last night and said he'll be picking me up. He's one of the few students at Villanova Prep who has his own car, and so it's a privilege to be seen in one.

I turn to the mirror by the stairs and take a look at myself one more time. Today is my first full day as Daven Porter's girlfriend, and I want to look absolutely perfect for him. I quickly ruffle a few fingers through my hair, combing through a few knots, when my phone rings, and it's Daven, telling me he's parked just around the corner. Mom and Dad still don't know about him. I told them I made some friends at school and am getting a ride with one of them. It's not technically a lie. They just happen to think the friend is a girl.

I grab my phone to send a short message back, telling him I'm on my way. Then I fish out my lip gloss from my bag and quickly polish my lips before smacking them to complete the look. Perfect. Well, as perfect as I can be.

"Bye, Mom! I'm heading out!" I call out to my mother in the kitchen.

"Stay safe, dear!" She yells back, followed by a few other words I missed as I shut the front door behind me.

I don't know why I feel so nervous. I mean,

Daven and I have kissed, and we're so comfortable around each other that I feel like we're best friends. But maybe part of me still has suspicions about him, that maybe this is all a game, and when I least expect it, he'll turn on me. No. I shake my head. He won't do that. He won't!

I ruffle my hair a bit more and unbutton a few more buttons of my blouse while heading over to where he's waiting. As I approach, he quickly gets out from his convertible and greets me with a long hug and a passionate kiss on the lips.

"You look stunning. Sexy as sexy can be," he whispers to me and pulls me into him once more.

"So do you," I whisper back.

"Oh, hey! I got something for you." I watch as he skips over to his car and pulls out a gift box. "Open it."

"What is it?" I ask.

"Just open it. You'll love it. Trust me."

Carefully, I undo the bow and open the red lid. Inside is a red and black wrist corsage with gold trimmings along the rim of the petals. "This is the most beautiful thing I've ever seen."

"And it's all for you." He takes the box from me, pulls out the corsage, and carefully places it around my wrist. "Bella Nova, will you do me the honor of going to the homecoming dance with me?"

A homecoming dance. I had never been to one before. It wasn't like my previous schools didn't have one; I was just never invited to one. Nor have I ever been invited to prom. But now, I have another chance. A chance to finally go to a school dance with, dare I say it? My boyfriend, the hottest guy in school, and he's all mine.

I try to contain my squeal, but as soon as he said those words, it all comes pouring out like a little girl in an ice cream store. But he found it charming, nonetheless, and I couldn't be happier.

When we arrive at school, he rushes over to open the passenger door for me, an act of a true gentleman. I can't wait to walk inside and see the mouth of the cheerleaders all drop at the corsage Daven had given me. Finally, I have something that the popular kids don't, and I love it.

"Hey, Daven." Stephanie approaches us as soon as we walk in. "Got a date to homecoming yet? I just bought the sexiest red strapless dress. Cost me nearly a grand, but it's totally worth it. I'm thinking I can get you a matching red suit to go along with it." She dances her fingers along his shoulder, but he quickly brushes them off.

Good.

"First of all, Stephanie, I'm not an accessory. And second, I already have a date. Bella."

He lifts up my hand and shows her the corsage. All the other girls gasp and rush over to admire the beautiful rose neatly placed on my wrist. Well, all but Stephanie.

"Her?! You're really choosing her, plain Jane, over me? Do you not realize that I'm the prettiest one on this entire campus? Guys literally trip over themselves to go out with me, and you're turning me down? For her?!"

Daven ponders over it for a moment, clearly playing along, and then finally answers, "Yup!" He turns to me. "Come on, Bella, let's go get the tickets. On me."

As we walk away, I can still hear Stephanie shouting behind us. "You're making a terrible mistake, Daven Porter! You'll regret turning me down! You'll regret it all!"

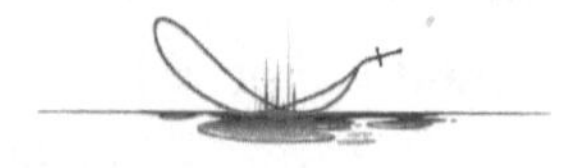

LATER THAT NIGHT, I kiss my corsage and place it down gently on my nightstand. Daven assured me that on the actual day of the dance, he'll replace it with a real one. He just wanted to get me one for now to show me how much he wants to be with me. Such a sweet guy. What will I ever do without him?

I yawn. I had stayed up to three in the morning studying for big test tomorrow, and I feel ready to crash and never wake up again. It only took seconds after my head hit the pillow for me to fall fast asleep.

"Bella, Bella Nova," a mysterious and deep voice calls out again.

I slowly open my eyes and find myself back on that squishy asphalt, my elbows burning as I lean them against the ground. "Ouch!"

"Who's out there?" I call out. "Show yourself! I'm tired of playing games."

Again, out of the corner of my eye, I see a dark figure, dark as midnight, an arm this time, and I follow it as it runs behind the same large rock.

"Gotcha!" I shout when I turn the corner and look behind the rock. Empty. No one's there. Damn it! I was so sure the animal had hidden here, and that I'd find it.

But when I turn back around, I see a monster, a tall and dark monstrous creature with midnight black skin and red eyes. Perched on the top of his head are large horns, resembling that of a ram. I want to scream, run away from the creature and pray for my life. But all that came out is a quiet yelp, followed by me slightly backing away.

The strange thing though, is that this monster is sort of... handsome? And I find myself extremely attracted to him, or it, or whatever it is. Is that weird? He looks so much like Daven! Maybe my immense attraction for Daven had manifested as a dream, and this monster is actually him.

"Who are you?" I ask again. "Daven? Is that you?"

The creature remains silent, but starts to walk over to me. I can't stop staring into his deep red eyes, eyes that look so perfect, pulling me in and enchanting me. Then he touches my face, and I can feel that part of it turning stiff before returning back to its natural state just seconds later.

"Daven?" I ask again.

But the creature shakes his head. "My name is Draven Asmodeus. I am a demon of the Under-world, and I need your help."

I nearly fall back at his words! "Underworld?"

"Hell."

I spring up on my bed, sweat pouring down my

forehead and neck. I look around, and I feel so relieved to find myself back in my own bedroom. The night is still dark, and when I look over at my phone, I still have two hours before the sun rises.

It's all just a dream. It's all just a dream. But even so, why did it feel so real? What the hell have I been eating lately? Ugh, I place a hand on my forehead. I really need to lay off those milkshakes at the diner. I never believed Mom when she told me I'm lactose sensitive. Maybe it's about time I do.

I sigh, rub a hand over my face and fingers on my eyes, and walk into the bathroom. There's definitely something going on with me. Never in my life have I had the same fictitious dream twice in a row. Turning on the faucet, I splash some cold water on my face and climb back into bed.

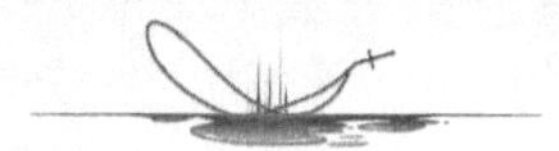

THE NEXT MORNING, I struggle to keep my eyes open when I met up with Daven. He already has a cup of coffee waiting for me, a true lifesaver, but even that isn't enough to keep me awake.

"What's wrong? You look like hell," he says when I walk up to him.

"Thanks..."

"Sorry, I didn't mean it like that. Are you okay? It looks like you haven't slept in days."

He hands me the coffee, and I take a long sip.

"I didn't really sleep well last night. I had a pretty scary nightmare, and it kept me up the rest of the night."

"I've had those before." He reaches over and wraps his arms around me. "And you know what usually helps me get through them?

"A tall glass of warm milk?"

Daven laughs. "That certainly helps! But I was going to say, calling someone. Finding someone to calm me down when I most need it, and ground me back to reality."

"How am I supposed to find someone to call in the dead of night?"

"Easy, me!" He caresses my face. "Bella, you know you can rely on me for anything, right? I love you."

"What?"

He blushes. "I meant to wait and tell you during the homecoming dance, to make it more special, but

I've wanted to say it for awhile now. Bella, I love you, ever since I first climbed onto that bus and saw you."

I can't believe my ears. Love? I've never experienced love before. Am I even capable of it?

"You don't have to say anything now," he continues. "But if you ever want to say it back, I'll be here."

"No, I do. I do want to say it because I feel it. I'm just afraid I'll mess it all up and scare you away."

He leans down and plants another passionate kiss on my lips. "Never. Nothing you do will ever scare me away. I love you, with everything I have."

"I love you, too."

That lights a spark in his eyes. "You have no idea how happy I am. What do you say we ditch school for a day and go to the beach, instead?"

"Are you crazy?? It's sixty degrees outside!" I cross my arms over my chest. "Besides, aren't you the one who said you'll never skip school?"

Daven shrugs, and then smiles at me. "I did, and yeah, it is. But there's something I want to show you. What do you say? Do you trust me?"

Mom would kill me if she ever finds out, but I can't help but give into those cute puppy dog eyes of his. "Let's do it."

"Awesome!" He grabs me by the waist and spins

me around, planting one more kiss on me before carrying me to his car.

Rincon Beach is a short thirty-minute drive away, a popular spot for tourists, and an even more popular spot for Daven whenever he needs to just get away. I love beaches, but growing up in Oregon, it was always too cold to visit one, even during the summer.

"Here, put this on," Daven turns and says to me after he pulls into the parking lot. He holds up a black blindfold and looks over at me with an expression on his face that says, "Trust me."

Immediately, flashbacks of Brick taking me to the abandoned farm pop into my head. The PTSD is no joke, and I vigorously start shaking my head. I don't even notice that my body is also trembling until Daven drops the blindfold and starts comforting me.

"It's okay, it's okay. I'm sorry, Bella. I didn't mean to offend you or hurt you or anything. I just thought it'd be a good way to surprise you. I'm so sorry. Are you okay?"

I nod, though my body still shaking.

"Tell you what, forget the blindfold. How about you just take my hand and close your eyes?"

"You're not going to kill me, are you?" I ask.

A wave of concern washes over his eyes, and I

can tell that he genuinely wasn't trying to hurt me. "I would never, ever, hurt you or betray you. You're my world now, and I only want what's best for you. If you can just trust me with this one thing, I promise you won't regret it."

"Okay," I whisper, taking his hand.

He leads me a few minutes down the beach, my feet sinking in the soft sand with every step, until we finally stop. With my eyes still closed, I can feel the cold breeze of the wind against my skin, and the slight touch of water against my feet as the waves wash up onto the shore.

"Almost there." I can hear him say, the smell of fish and crab reminding me of when I used to sit by the dock back home in Astoria. "Okay," he says again. "Open your eyes."

I slowly open my eyes and am shocked by what I'm seeing. Roses scattered over the sand, forming a large heart, and in the middle, a bottle of champagne and some chocolate-covered strawberries placed on top of a blanket.

"Did... did you do this?" I turn around to ask Daven, who had magically pulled a bouquet of roses from behind his back.

"Ditching school was my plan all along. I was just praying for you to say yes so all this wouldn't go to waste. I drove here this morning before picking you up to set everything up. Do you like it?"

I'm at a loss for words. Daven's treating me like a princess, and part of me still feels like I don't deserve it. I have never been treated like such a queen before, and I still don't know how to act when someone does surprise me.

"I... I love it, but you didn't have to do all this."

"I know, but I wanted to, because you're special." He walks over behind me and wraps his arms around me, snuggling his face into my neck and breathing softly on my chest. "I love you so much, Bella."

Oh, no, not again. I can feel my panties getting wet from his touch, and I can hear my mother in the back of my head telling me to run away if I want to stay out of prison. But it's too late. My body's already melting into his arms as he slowly and softly kisses my neck.

"I want you, Bella," he whispers into my ear and starts to unbutton my blouse.

I let him continue. I don't want to stop him, even though I know I should. This is Brick Cannon and Alex Shaw all over again, but I don't care. My mind is too far gone, and it's time for my body to speak. He strips me down to expose my bra, letting my blouse fall onto the sand, and caresses my cleavage with his gentle hands before smoothing them up my back and undoing the clasp.

"You're perfect," he whispers again and lays me down on the blanket, encircling my breasts with his tongue before unzipping my skirt and grazing a hand up and down my inner thigh, running his fingers over the bite marks with no questions asked. I feel like I'm in Heaven.

And when he undresses himself and pulls me on top of him, my thighs rubbing against his as our bodies connect into one, I feel like I can finally die happy. He feels so warm inside of me, and the sounds coming from his mouth makes me want him more because I know he wants me.

"I love you, Bella, forever and ever," he heaves as his body continues to jerk in a repetitive motion, and moments later, we both collapse into each other in a state of ecstasy, lying naked on the beach, skin to skin, still connected.

"So, tell me about this dream. What's it about that's gotten you so worked up?" he asks, reaching over for the bottle of champagne and pouring us both a glass.

"Honestly, I don't even know where to start, but I've had the same dream for two days in a row now. And it's some sort of monster with black skin, says he's from Hell, and he needs my help. It's really freaky."

"That *is* freaky," Daven agrees. "Usually, my nightmares are about falling off a tall building or getting run over by a car. I don't think I've ever heard of a dream about a creature from Hell asking for help."

"What do you think it means? Is it bad?"

He shakes his head. "Nah, I think you're just stressed out, or tired. It'll go away soon. I'm sure it's nothing to worry about. Just take deep breaths before you fall asleep." Then he grabs my hand. "But if it comes up again, I'm just one phone call away."

AND SO, that night, I spend ten whole minutes breathing, in and out, in and out, in and out, until I finally breathe myself to sleep. At first, it seems to work, waking up in a French restaurant, wearing a sequin red dress, and being seated at a cloth table in front of Daven, who's dressed in a crisp black suit with a red striped tie.

"Cheers," he says. "To our eight-year anniversary."

"Good evening, sir and madam. My name is Jean Pierre, and I'll be your waiter today. Can I get you started with something to drink?"

"Two glasses of Merlot, please." Daven winks at me. "It's her favorite."

"Coming right up, sir. And would you like to hear about the specials for tonight?"

"Lay 'em on us."

"For the appetizer, we have slow-poached escargots with garlic sauce. The soup for tonight is tomato and fennel, and for the main course, we have the most delicious serving of freshly-caught help me."

I shake my head, taking a minute to register what he had just said. "I'm sorry, what's the main course?" I ask.

"I shall repeat, madam. For the main course, we have the most delicious serving of freshly-caught HELP ME!"

Suddenly, the room starts to shake.

"Daven! What's happening?" I call out.

But instead of the usual comforting voice of Daven reassuring me that everything will be okay, his face begins to melt, revealing nothing but a skeletal structure beneath it. His eyes liquify, and his lips, the lips I had grown fond of kissing, dissolve into a pile of ashes on the tablecloth. The room starts to spin, around and around, all the tables and chairs flying around the room, right before the entire thing gets suctioned into a massive black hole.

And here I am again, finding myself back on that squishy asphalt with the temperature of a whistling kettle. The breathing didn't work. Whatever other crappy advice Daven probably has up his sleeve most likely won't work. It just seems like no matter that I do, I'll always just end up in Hell.

"Welcome back, Bella," the monster named Draven walks out from behind the rock. "I've been expecting you."

"Who are you? And what do you want from me?" I shout, the sound of my voice echoing in the cave.

"You're the chosen one, the one our leader has prophesized would come and finally save us, finally set us free. You are the only one who can help us."

As he speaks, his red eyes glow an even brighter red, as if they're opening up and sucking me in. I force myself to look away, to claw myself toward the opposite direction, but no matter how much I try, the monster is just too powerful.

"I can't help you! I can't! I can't even help

myself. Please, whoever you are, leave me alone! Leave me alone! Leave me alone!"

I wake up, covered in sweat. I look over at my phone and sigh that it's only 2am. Another horrible dream. Why does this keep happening? I've never been a fan of horror movies, and I haven't seen one since I was in the fifth grade. I don't understand why I keep having these recurring nightmares.

"I'm just one phone call away." I hear Daven saying in my head. "Night or day, you can always call me."

I reach over for the phone, but then stop. No, I can't. I can't bother him. He needs his sleep. But if I don't, and he finds out that I didn't, he'll be just as angry that I didn't ask for help.

It takes barely two rings before Daven answers.

"Hello? Bella? Is that you?"

"I had another dream," I whisper, trying to avoid waking up my parents.

It's bad enough that I'm up so late on a school night. I can't have them finding out that I'm on the phone with a boy.

Daven's tired voice becomes more alert. "The same dream? Are you okay? What happened?"

"The monster. It just kept saying how I'm destined to save him, how I'm the chosen one. And the red eyes! They're so bright, like they're sucking in my soul. I don't know what to do, Daven. It all just feels so real, and I'm afraid to go back to sleep. What if it's trying to tell me something?"

"I'm sorry, Bella. I wish I'm there in bed with you. So, I can hold you and keep you safe. But my father will kill me if he finds out I'm gone."

"I understand. So will mine."

"But, hey, if you can somehow make it through the night, I promise, tomorrow, we'll go see a psychiatrist. My family knows a great one. Super experienced. He helped my mom get over her post-partum depression after my sister was born. I'm sure he'll have an answer to your dreams. I'm here with you, Bella. I won't let anything happen to you."

"Thanks, Daven. That means a lot. I wish I could kiss you right now."

He starts to make sounds of kissing noises through the phone, which makes me giggle. "When I pick you up tomorrow, I promise to shower you with kisses."

"I look forward to them. Night, Daven."

"Goodnight, Bella. I love you."

I hang up the phone and lie back down against my pillow. I just have to get through the next four hours without falling asleep, and tomorrow, I'll get answers. Just four hours. I can do it, right? I manage to talk myself into calming down a bit, doing whatever I need to just get through the night. And just when I finally start to doze off again, I hear a voice.

"Hello, Bella."

"Whoa!" I nearly leap out of bed at the sound of the voice, grabbing my phone and turning on the flashlight.

At first, there's nothing there. Nothing but the same old bedroom I had grown accustomed to. I slowly shift my light from one side of the room to the other. Nothing. Nothing. And then out of nowhere, I see dark skin, large horns, the creature! He's in my room! But how?!

I want to scream, but I quickly throw my hands over my mouth instead. I thought it was only a dream. What the hell is this?! I start sweating bullets as the creature comes closer to me, and I nearly shit myself when he sits down on my bed.

"Please leave me alone," I whisper quietly, pulling my blanket over half my face.

I close my eyes, squeezing them tight and hoping that it's all part of my wild imagination. Maybe if I count to ten, he'll go away. No twenty. That would be better.

Twenty seconds later, I open my eyes, and he's

gone. My room is completely empty again, with no traces of anyone breaking and entering. I let out a sigh of relief. It's just my imagination. It's just my imagination. But all of a sudden, a dark hand grabs onto my left wrist, pulling me down, before I finally kick it and pull away, and the room falls quiet again.

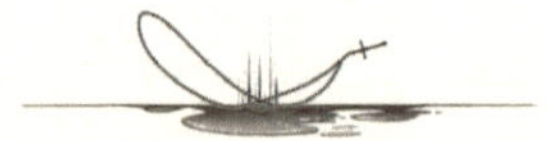

THE NEXT MORNING, my eyes hurt from staying up all night. Part of me still isn't sure whether the whole thing was a dream or just a hallucination. It can't be real. There's no such thing as monsters. Maybe it's finally time to lay off the sugar. A chocolate bar everyday can't be good for me.

I throw the sheets off my body, grab a towel, and walk into the bathroom to shower. When I pull the sweater off over my head, I notice a mark on my left wrist. Not just any mark, but the mark of a large monstrous hand.

"No," I whisper, dropping my towel onto the tiled floor. "No, what? No!"

Throwing my sweater back on, I hug my body

close. What's happening to me? Why do I keep seeing things that aren't there?

I jump when my phone starts to ring. It's Daven.

"Hello?"

"Hey, babe, are you doing better? You seemed pretty worked up last night."

"Not really. I think I really do need to go see that psychiatrist. I feel like I'm seeing things."

"Well, you're in luck! I was able to book you an appointment for today. I'll take you over after school. And don't worry, I'll be there with you the entire time."

"Thanks, Daven. You're the best." I smile, briefly taking my mind away from the mark on my wrist.

Daven truly is the best. He's no Brick Cannon. He's no Alex Shaw. He's no Billy Styles. He's simply perfect.

"I love you, Bella."

"I love you, too."

As I hang up, I see something move behind me.

"Mom? Ace? Is someone there?" I call out.

But there's no answer. Mom and Dad should've gone to work by now, and Ace never comes to my room unless it's absolutely necessary.

"Who's there?" I call out again.

Still no answer. I must be losing it.

I walk over to my bathroom sink. Maybe a splash of cold water will clear things up for me. The feeling of the cold against my skin feels so refreshing, so calming. Maybe this is what I needed all along. I then reach over to grab a towel to wipe my face dry, rubbing the soft cotton into my forehead and below my eyes.

"What the fuck is that?" I suddenly yell when I look at my reflection in the mirror.

Close behind me, I see him, the monster, the creature from Hell. His skin black as ash, and his massive horns perched on top of his six-foot body.

Quickly, I throw the towel back over my face and rub as hard as I can.

"It's not real. It's not real." I keep repeating to myself, and when I look back at the mirror, he's gone.

CHAPTER 5

When I turn the corner of my street, Daven's standing there, as always, with a cup of coffee and a breakfast bagel in his hands. He greets me with a kiss on the cheek and a light, gentle hug.

"You look like you've just seen a monster," he jokes.

"That's not funny. You don't know what it's been like," I jab back.

"You're right, I'm sorry. That was insensitive." He hands me the paper bag. "I got you your favorite. Bacon, egg, and cheese on an everything bagel. Call this my peace offering?"

My heart melts. He remembered. "Done."

"Dr. Schultz is a legend when it comes to deciphering dreams. I'm sure he can figure out what's going on with you in no time!"

"Let's hope so. I don't know how much longer I can go without sleep."

I finish off the rest of my bagel and climb into Daven's car. The feeling of the breezy wind against my hair feels relaxing, like soft nails are massaging my head. It brings back such wonderful memories of when Mom used to brush my hair and braid it when I was a little girl, a feeling I never want to end.

I turn my head to the side to get more comfortable, catching my reflection in the side mirror... along with the reflection of the creature.

"Shit!" I jump, nearly knocking an arm into Daven, who almost loses control of the wheel.

We begin swerving down the road, Daven trying hard to steady the convertible as I continue shaking beside him. When he finally manages to pull over onto the nearest sidewalk, my heart is still pounding heavily from the initial shock.

"Jesus, Bella! What was that?" he exclaims.

I can tell that he's frustrated, angry even, and I don't blame him.

"I saw it! Him! The monster! He's in the mirror!"

"Where?"

I point over to the sideview mirror where the creature had appeared, but when Daven walks around to take a look, all we can see are our own reflections.

"I don't see anything, babe. Are you sure he was here?"

"I swear! I saw him! The dark skin. The large horns. There's no way I could've mistaken that!"

Daven sighs. "Whatever it was, it's gone now. Let me know if he comes back, though. That meeting with Dr. Schultz can't come soon enough."

I watch, feeling stupid, as Daven walks back around to the driver's side. Am I just hallucinating? It has to be the lack of sleep. I'm just seeing things! It has to be!

Daven continues down the road, and I try to rest my head again, feeling the soft nails massage against my scalp. It's so peculiar how wind can do that. A little too peculiar. I glance over at the side mirror again, and find long black nails attached to long black fingers massaging through my hair and caressing the top of my head. I quickly jerk away, blink several times, but the creature is still there, sitting behind me, staring at me, and grinning.

He's not going away. Why isn't he going away? I blink several more times. I look over at Daven, who has finally regained control of the car. I can't bother him with this again. He'll crash, and it'll be all my fault. I can't have the death of yet another person on my hands. Instead, I fish out my sunglasses from my backpack and pop them on. If I don't see the creature, then he doesn't exist.

"I HAVE a few council meetings today to prepare for the dance on Friday, so I won't be around much. But I'll meet you here after school, okay? So, we can head over together," Daven says to me when we pull up to the school parking lot.

"Sure."

I would rather have Daven by my side at all times. Who knows when this creature will pop up again? But he'd been so sweet and caring thus far, and I'd rather not be an impediment on him.

He gives me a light kiss on the cheek and skips off into a separate building.

When I walk into the main building, Stephanie and her crew are already there by their lockers, polishing off each other's lipstick and comparing the levels of fat on their thighs.

"Well, well, look who we have here! Plain Jane without her shiny knight? What's wrong, Plain Jane? Daven dump you already?" Stephanie begins to taunt.

"Leave me alone," I reply quietly.

"You know, I bet Daven didn't tell you this, but we hooked up yesterday," she continues.

That's when I stop. "What?"

"Ah, so he definitely didn't tell you. It's true, and my girls here can back me up." She points to the crew behind her, who all nod in a robotic motion. "He came over to my house last night, snuck in, and we fucked on my bed." She holds up two fingers. "Twice."

"You're lying. Daven would never do that. He doesn't even like you."

Stephanie laughs. "Well, that's not what he told me last night. The best he ever had, he told me."

My rage begins to build, fists clenching. My entire body is telling me to punch her in her perfect little face and break her perfect little nose.

But suddenly, he appears again, his reflection shining in the mirror behind Stephanie, stroking my hair. I jump and back up against the lockers.

"Stay away from me! Stay away from me!" I start crying.

Of course, this only provokes Stephanie and her little army of blondes to laugh at me even more.

"Wow, Daven really did choose the wrong person. Look at her! She's crazy!"

Sweating bullets, I push past her and bolt down the hallway, running as fast as I can from a creature that I can't even see anymore. I keep going until I reach the girl's restroom. I kick open a stall and drop down to my knees, crying into my hands and praying that it all ends.

And then I hear a knock. I freeze, unsure of who it is or whether they'd heard me. I pull off a wad of toilet paper and hold it against my nose, breathing into it to avoid making any loud sounds.

I hear the knock again, more aggressive this time. What if it's the creature? What if he's come to take me? I hold my breath, shrinking into a ball in an attempt to hide myself.

Then I hear a voice. "Bella?"

Daven! It's Daven. I jump to my feet and unlock the stall.

"Bella, it's me, Daven. Can you please open up?"

I rush over to the main door and unlock it.

"Daven!" I throw my arms around him, holding him close to me, though my body is still shaking.

"Bella, what happened? One minute, I'm in the main office, and the next, I see you running down the hallway. Are you okay?"

My tears continue to drip onto his hands as he caresses my face, forehead to forehead, and he pulls me even closer to him.

"I keep... I keep seeing him. The monster! He won't leave me alone. Make him go away, Daven! Make him go away!"

"Shh, it's okay, Bella. Just breathe. I'm here now. You're safe."

Daven excused himself from the rest of his classes so he could stay with me the rest of the day in the nurse's office. He thought it's some kind of fever, the rise in temperature making me hallucinate things that aren't there, but when Nurse Mary checked me out, I was completely fine. Healthy as the average person.

"You doing okay, Bella? We only have an hour

left, and then we can head over to Dr. Schultz." Daven turns to me and grabs my hands with his. "Everything will be okay."

I nod. "Thanks for staying with me. I don't know how I could've made it through the day without you."

"Of course, babe. I love you. I'll always be here for you."

Then I remember what Stephanie had said. "Daven, can I ask you something?"

"Anything you want."

"Did... did you have sex with Stephanie?"

A look of horror washes over his face. "What? Of course not! I'd never do that, even if I weren't with you. Where did you hear that?"

"She told me this morning. Said you went over to her house last night, and that you said she's the best you ever had."

"Bella, Bella, Bella. Stephanie is a liar. A Class A liar. I was home all night with my parents, worried sick about you. I barely even fell asleep because I was expecting a call from you. Don't believe a word she says. Besides, *you're* the best I've ever had. Actually, you're the only girl I've ever been with." He blushes.

"Really? I'm your first?"

He nods. "That's embarrassing, isn't it? But my

family is incredibly religious, and I've just been saving myself for the right person. You."

I shake my head. "No, it's not embarrassing. Now, I feel ashamed for not trusting you, and for not being a virgin."

"It's alright, babe. I understand. The important thing is that we leave the past in the past and just move forward. And you can always ask me anything. I won't be offended."

"I love you, Daven." I lean in and kiss him, his lips so warm that I never want to let go.

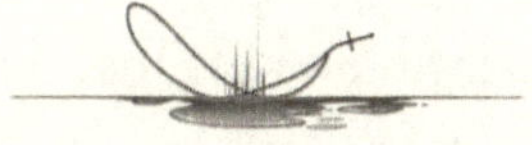

LESS THAN TWO HOURS LATER, I find myself sitting on a beige couch in Dr. Schultz's office. Daven, of course, is right there next to me, his arm wrapped around my waist as if he never wants to let me go. I glance around the room. Everything looks good so far. A certificate awarded to Barry Schultz from UCLA, dozens upon dozens of books on his bookcase on multiple personalities and schizophrenic disorders, and best of all, no monsters to be seen.

"Hanging in there?" Daven asks.

I smile at him, right when the door opens, and an elderly man in his sixties, wearing a bolo tie and carrying a large textbook, walks in.

"Ms. Nova, I presume?" I nod as he looks at me before sitting down. "And Mr. Porter, how nice to see you again."

"Dr. Schultz, thank you so much again for agreeing to see us. How's your son doing? Parker, is it?" Daven asks.

"Oh, that kid is so unmotivated that sometimes I wonder if he's got a loose screw in there. It'll be a miracle if he manages to make it through middle school."

"Give it time. Some kids just develop faster than others. I'm sure little Parker will start shaping up soon enough."

"Let's just hope so." Dr. Schultz then turns to me. "So, enough time wasted. Bella, what brings you in today? Daven here says you've been dealing with some bad nightmares."

"Worse than just nightmares. I think they're haunting me."

He leans back in his chair and rubs his pointer finger and thumb against his beard. "Haunting you? Interesting. I haven't heard that one before. Tell me more about that."

I look over at Daven, who mouths, "It's okay."

"There's this creature, a monster of some sort, in my dreams. He has black skin like tar, large horns, and he keeps saying he's from Hell. At first, I thought it was just a dream. Things usually got better once I wake up. But lately, I start seeing him in my reflection wherever I go. In the mirror of Daven's car, in the mirror at school. It's like this monster is following me, even when I'm not asleep."

"What do you think it is, doc?" Daven asks.

"Hmm, it *is* very peculiar, and Bella here is definitely experiencing some sort of hallucination. Bella, have you ever been diagnosed with schizophrenia? It's usually brought on by childhood trauma or excessive drug use."

"I've never used drugs, and I don't—" I stop. Trauma, he had said. What if my PTSD is what's causing all of this?

"Bella, you okay?" Daven must've noticed me drifting off into space.

"It seems that Bella here suddenly remembers something. A past childhood trauma, perhaps?" Dr. Schultz starts to say.

I begin heaving. All those memories I'd tried so hard to suppress come rushing back. The gunshot. The blood. Brick.

"Doc, I think we're going to have to come back another time. Thanks for all your help," Daven informs Dr. Schultz before leading me out the door. He grips tightly onto my hand and slowly walks me out. "Oh, yeah, feel free to bill the card on file."

"Will do. Come back anytime, Bella. My door is always open."

I continue to heave, even as we walk out of Schultz's office. "He can't help me," I cry out to Daven. "No one can help me!"

"Don't say that, Bella. This was only your first session. No one's first session goes well. We'll try again another day. But right now, I think we need to get you home so you can rest."

The entire drive back to my place, the both of us remain silent. I didn't feel like talking, and Daven could sense it, giving me my space. I feel so mentally drained, like the monster had somehow sucked out all the energy inside me.

"Daven," I turn my head over to face him. "Am I a burden to you?" I ask.

"Are you kidding me? Of course not! You can never be a burden. I'm here for you, remember? You need help, and I want to be there for you. Don't ever think that you're impeding me."

"But wouldn't you rather be with someone with less problems? Maybe someone like Stephanie?"

He pulls to a park around the corner of my house, where he usually stops, and turns to me. "Bella, I know whatever Stephanie said to you probably got to your head, but you need to stop self-doubting. I'm with you. You! If I didn't want to be, I wouldn't be here right now, okay? But the important thing now is that you get some sleep."

"But I can't. What if I see... the thing again?"

Daven pauses for a moment. He looks so cute whenever he's serious. "How about you spend the night at my place? My folks won't mind. Just tell your parents that you're staying at a friend's."

He has a point. Ever since I met Daven, Mom has been under the impression that I'd made several female friends at school. She never questions it. And with her attention focused on Ace and his failing grades lately, I don't think she'll mind.

"Sure," I answer. "I'll call my parents on the way. I'm sure they won't mind."

He plants a kiss on my cheek and pulls out of park.

The Porters only live twenty minutes away from my house, and when Daven pulls up into the driveway, my jaw nearly drops. The house is massive!

Like a mansion on steroids! But I guess being the mayor of an entire town, Cliff Porter can't risk ruining his reputation by living in a shitty town home.

Daven hops out of the car and shuffles around to open the passenger door for me. He then helps me get up and wraps an arm around my waist, probably to keep me from falling over with how unstable I've been.

As Daven leads me into the mansion, he waves to the gardener, who's manning the most beautiful bed of flowers I've ever seen. And when the maid opens the front double doors, I'm greeted with a magnificent sparkling chandelier, a double spiral staircase, and a hardwood floor shiny enough to eat off of.

"Your house is amazing," I whisper to Daven, who tucks me closer under his arm.

"It *is* pretty extravagant, isn't it? My parents like to go all out when showcasing their status and wealth. Me, personally, I like to keep things minimal. Less is more, I always say."

"Daven! Is that you?" A female voice yells out, and a petite blonde woman, probably only about fifteen years older than me, appears in front of us.

"Mother." Daven reaches over and gives her a

hug. "I want you to meet my girlfriend, Bella. She's staying over tonight. I hope that's okay."

His mother. Jackie Porter. She's so beautiful. Like all the cheerleaders in school merged into one person. I'd seen her on the news before, alongside Cliff, but given her age, I had always assumed that she's Cliff's secretary, not his wife.

"Of course, dear!" She turns to me. "Bella Nova, it's so good to finally meet you! Daven's told me so much about you. Oh, you're such a cute girl. No wonder my son snatched you right up."

"Mom, you're embarrassing me!"

"Oh, Daven, he gets embarrassed by his parents way too easily."

"It's alright, Mrs. Porter. It's really nice to meet you."

"And so polite!" She places a hand on her chest, over where her heart is. "Dinner will be ready in about two hours. Bella, which do you prefer, salmon or tilapia? It's seafood night!"

The choice in dinner is such a new concept to me. Back home, it's always, "eat what's on the table, or don't eat at all." And leftovers are usually the only choice.

"Salmon sounds good," I answer.

"Good choice! That's my little Daven's favorite,

too. Now, go enjoy yourselves until then. But oh! Not too much!"

"Mom!" Daven hisses.

He grabs my hand and leads me up the stairs toward his room.

"Sorry about my mother. She can be a little... optimistic."

"It's fine. I don't mind. My mom's usually the same around guests. I like her. She's nice."

"Daven!" A little girl, no more than ten, rushes down the stairs to us. "You'll never guess what happened at school today. Some smelly boy stuck gum in my hair. Gum! And it took mother a hundred hours to get it off!"

Daven laughs and turns to me. "Bella, meet my little sister, CeCe."

"Hi, CeCe, it's nice to meet you."

Daven leans down to the still pouty girl. "And CeCe, you know that when a boy messes with you, it means he likes you, right?"

"Ew, no! I don't like boys! They stink!"

Daven chuckles.

CeCe turns to me. "Hi, Bella. Are you Daven's girlfriend? He talks about you all the time and how pretty you are. You're really pretty."

Now, it's my turn to smile. His entire family is so

charming. Now, I see where he gets it from. "I am, and thank you. You're really pretty, too."

CeCe blushes.

"Mom's making fish for dinner tonight. You better go tell her what you want before she gets started."

"Fish?! I HATE fish!" CeCe exclaims and bolts down the stairs.

"She's a bit of a drama queen; don't mind her." Daven wraps his arm back around me, and we continue up the stairs.

"She's cute."

Then he leans over and kisses me. "Not as cute as you."

Walking into his bedroom, I struggle to believe that his room is part of the house. Everything else inside the house is so extravagant and shiny. But in Daven's room, his gray walls and navy-blue sheets aren't much to look at. And in the center, sitting on his desk, sits a picture frame of the two of us when we went to Rincon Beach. We look so happy together, truly in love.

I pick it up and run a thumb over our faces. "Wow, you weren't kidding when you said you like to keep things minimalistic."

He comes up behind me and wraps his arms

around my body, kissing my neck and making me swoon. "Ha, yeah, and that picture right there is my most prized possession."

I spin around, and my lips meet his. He pulls me in by the waist, and we lock lips, tasting each other like we were both starving. He takes off my blazer, dropping it to the floor, before returning his hands back up and unbuttoning my blouse.

"Won't your mom hear us?" I briefly stop him.

"Nah, she always cooks with the music blasting. She won't hear a thing," he assures me and gently leans me down against his bed.

LATER THAT NIGHT, when the rest of the house is asleep, Daven sleeping soundly next to me with his arm still around my bare body, I look around. Even in the comfort of my boyfriend's arms, I'm struggling to fall asleep, terrified of the monster in my nightmare returning.

"Hey, Daven," I softly whisper, waking him up.

"Huh? Bella, what is it?"

"I can't fall asleep. What if the creature comes back?"

"If he does, I'll beat the crap out of him."

"Can you stay up with me for a little longer? Please?"

He sits up a little. "Alright, anything for my girl. Any thoughts on how to keep us occupied?"

"I think I have an idea."

I lean over to him, grabs his face, and paints his neck and chest with my lips. I can hear him slightly moan at the pleasure, right before he grabs my body and flips me over.

Minutes later, Daven is fast asleep, and I find myself alone once again. I begin to doze off, my vision going in and out, until I eventually fall fast asleep alongside him.

"Bella, Bella Nova." I hear a deep, dark voice call out.

I keep my eyes closed. I can already tell who it is. The squishy texture below me certainly doesn't tell me otherwise.

"Why? Why do you keep bothering me? Why do you keep coming into my dreams? What do you want from me? Just leave me alone!"

The creature comes out from behind the rock.

But this time, he looks innocent, scared even, like I'm the monster, not him.

"Bella, please, listen to me. I need your help. My family needs your help."

"I can't help you. I can't! Find someone else, please!"

"Bella! Wake up! Wake up!"

I find myself being shaken awake. My eyes open, happy to see Daven's naked bedroom.

I throw my arms around him, shaking. "I saw him again. He keeps saying he needs me to save him. Him and his family. I can't save him. I can't save anyone!"

I break down in Daven's arms, crying my eyes out as he comforts me the rest of the night.

CHAPTER 6

Friday's finally here, and it took Daven days of convincing for me to agree to attend homecoming. Mom even took me shopping to buy me a brand-new dress, a long black sequin halter dress with the back bare, sexy yet elegant at the same time.

Dr. Schultz had given me a small bottle of sleep

medication. Well, he'd given it to Daven. I was too busy avoiding monsters to get it. It won't solve my problem, but it's enough to get me through a few nights without completely collapsing.

And the monster. I started seeing him less and less, probably because of the medication. Either that, or he'd gone back to Hell and decided to leave me alone. As long as I stop seeing him, I couldn't care less which option it was.

As I'm getting ready, my phone rings. It's a call from Daven. "I can't wait to pick you up, beautiful."

That's another thing. My parents finally found out about Daven, not that we're dating. No, of course not. But that he's my date for the dance. When they first saw him, they were both shocked that I'm going out with the mayor's son. My father, being the political person that he is, turned their interview into a debate about whether the laws in this town accommodate all races and ages. It was humiliating! But Daven handled it well. He handles everything well. It's why I love him. He keeps me grounded when I'm floating through the air of my own hot head.

"Me, too," then I hang up and walk over to the mirror to put on my makeup. I usually like to keep it pretty natural. A bit of gloss on my lips and some eyeliner. Nothing too fancy. My mother always said

I have a natural beauty, and Daven seems to like me just as I am.

As I sit in front of my vanity, lining my lips with the strawberry pink gloss and dousing my wrist with concealer to cover up the monstrous hand print that still resides there, I see a shadow in the corner, coming from my closet. Then I shake my head. I'm just being paranoid. It's probably just a shirt or something.

I look away, but when I quickly glance back at it, the shadow almost looks humanlike, with... with horns? I whip my head around and grab the purple umbrella sitting beside me. Holding the handle up, I slowly make my way over to the closet door. On the count of three, I lift up my foot and kick the door open, only to see my jacket fall off its hanger. A wave of relief washes over me. It's just my clothes. Nothing to worry about. I'm definitely just being paranoid.

I hear the doorbell ring, followed by the sound of my mom's voice. "Bella! Daven's here!"

"Coming!" I call back.

I walk over to my vanity once more and open the drawer to grab a pair of matching earrings, the black pearl ones, to be exact. But beside them, I see my sapphire necklace, the same one that Brick had given me a week before I killed him.

It was my birthday, and we picked up a box of pepperoni pizza to eat together at a park, when he took out the smallest gift box, and inside, was the sapphire necklace. I thought it was the most beautiful piece of jewelry I had ever laid my eyes on, though I haven't seen much during my lifetime. And although every time I see this necklace, I get only bad memories, I still can't find it in myself to throw it away. It has too much sentimental value; I'd rather just hide it behind the rest of my valuables.

Walking down the stairs, I can already hear Dad chatting it up with Daven about his father the mayor. My dad is a hardcore liberal in a very conservative town, and he usually has much to tell people, even if they don't want to hear it. I can tell that Daven's getting uncomfortable, but he's too polite to ask my father to stop.

"Dad!" I interrupt them. "Daven and I should really get going. We don't want to be late."

Daven's mouth drops open when he stands up and sees me standing by the door. He immediately walks over, ready to give me a kiss, but settles for a long hug instead when I remind him that my parents still don't know we're dating.

"You look so gorgeous," he whispers, pinning the real corsage on my dress.

I mouth a "thanks" and wrap an arm around his waist while my mother snaps a few pictures. Five in, and I realize I have to stop her. If no one does, she usually goes overboard.

"That's enough, Mom. We should really get going."

"Aww, my baby is finally going to her first dance! This is such an exciting moment!" Then she looks at Daven. "Take care of her. Bring her back by nine."

"Yes, ma'am." Daven salutes.

As I follow him to his car, I can't stop staring at how good he looks. The freshly pressed suit really fits him well, accentuating his tone body and muscular arms.

"Your parents seem nice," he says, waiting for me to catch up to him. "Where's Ace? He going to the dance to?"

I shake my head. "Dances aren't really his thing. I'm pretty sure he's hanging out in someone's basement getting high right now."

"Stoner kid, got it. I'm glad you're not into that type of thing."

"And what if I were?"

He smirks. "I guess I'll have to dump your ass."

"Oh, stop it." I hit him lightly with my purse.

"By the way," he leans in and whispers. "You have no idea how much I want to rip that dress off your body. You look so sexy in it."

He pulls the car around the corner after we get in, away from my parents' sight, and kisses me hard on the lips, his gentle hands running up and down my bare back.

"What do you say we just skip the dance and go back to my place?"

"I'd love to, but don't you have to be there? Make sure nothing goes wrong?"

He stops kissing me, and his face drops. "Damn, you're right. After then? I rip that dress off you?"

"Anything you want."

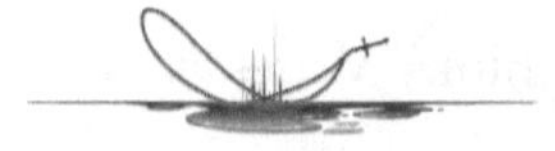

HUNDREDS OF STUDENTS are already standing in the gymnasium when we arrive. Some on the dance floor, while others linger awkwardly by the punch bowl. Gold and black decorations line the room, and bright disco lights sway back and forth. I see Stephanie and her group of cheerleaders at first glance. It wasn't hard, especially when they marched up to Daven and started flirting with him as soon as we walked in.

"Hey, Daven," Stephanie sings. "Like my dress? As you can see, the neckline perfectly lines my cleavage." She winks at him.

"It's alright." Then he turns to me. "I have to run backstage and check on the band. Are you okay without me for a bit?"

"Yeah, but hurry up! I want to dance with you."

"I'll be as quick as a bunny." He kisses me on the cheek and runs off, leaving me with none other than Stephanie.

She let out a breath of air. "You know, Bella, is it? I want to apologize for my behavior toward you. Honestly, I was a little jealous that Daven chose you over me, but I'm starting to come to my senses. And you're not that bad. I'd like to start over. Truce?" she asks, reaching out her hand.

"Are you serious?"

I'm skeptical. Of course, I am! Stephanie and the rest of her crew has done nothing but harass and humiliate me ever since my first day at Villanova Prep. It's hard believing that she'd want to stop now. But then I think about Daven and what he would do. Daven has the soul of an angel, and if he were in my shoes, he'd forgive her. Be the bigger person. It's what Daven would want me to do.

"If I weren't serious, I wouldn't be extending my hand to you. I don't need to touch other people's germs for nothing."

I roll my eyes. "Fine, truce." And I reach out my own hand to shake hers.

"Perfect!" she exclaims. "Because I actually have a little gift for you. It's my way of saying sorry, and that I hope you, and Daven, will forgive me. In fact, I hope that we can become friends. You know, sit together during lunch, go shopping after school, girl stuff. Wouldn't that be fun?"

I wince. Girl stuff? It's never been something I've gotten into. I'd much rather hop on my laptop and binge away my favorite television series. But after everything that happened with Chelsea, I can use a new set of friends, friends I don't end up screwing over.

"I guess." I force a soft smile.

I follow them to where they had placed a large beautifully wrapped pink gift box. I wonder what it is, what could possibly fit inside something like that. Part of me wants to turn the other way. I still don't trust Stephanie. But the other part knows I should, that the reason I'm such a loner is because I don't trust people. And so, I walk over, untie the bow, and open the box.

And out sprays a foul concoction of rotten milk, mustard, and a brown liquid that I hope to God isn't dog shit.

I scream as the mixture covers my brand-new dress and squirts all over my face, the stench of the blend enough to make me vomit. Why did I trust her? I should've known better than to believe in someone who's been out to get me since day one.

Without even waiting for Daven, I turn around and rush out the door. I can hear Daven calling out after me, but I refuse to stop. Right now, I don't want anything to do with anyone, not even Daven.

I didn't stop until I ran all the way home. Mom and Dad had gone out to dinner, and I open the door to an empty home. Quickly, I rush up the stairs and into my shower, turning on the water and allowing it to drench my entire body, clothes included. Tears pour nonstop from my eyes. My heart feels so broken and betrayed, and I shrink down into the corner of my bathtub, hugging myself and praying that my life ends.

My phone starts to ring when I walk out of the bathroom. Daven. Seven missed calls and counting. But I just ignore him. After the humiliation I went through, I can't trust anyone. Not even him. For all I know, he could've been behind it the whole time. He could've been playing me and on Stephanie's side. They're all against me. Even him.

I walk into my closet and throw on an old sweatshirt before climbing into bed. My phone rings again. Daven. I turn it off. It's something I'll deal with whenever I feel like it. I reach over to my lamp and switch off the light. Nice and cozy, dark and quiet. Just the way I like it. And just when I begin to doze off, I hear a voice.

"Bella Nova, save me."

UNLEASHING HELL BOOK ONE

FINDING HIM

VIOLA TEMPEST